Oh, What a Thanksgiving!

by STEVEN KROLL • Illustrated by S.D. SCHINDLER

SCHOLASTIC INC.

New York Toronto London Auckland Sydney

For my family
—SK

ISBN 0-590-44874-9

Text copyright © 1988 by Steven Kroll.

Illustrations copyright © 1988 by S.D. Schindler.

All rights reserved. Published by Scholastic Inc.

BLUE RIBBON is a registered trademark of Scholastic Inc.

12 11 10 9 8 7 6 5 4 3   2 3 4 5 6/9

Printed in the U.S.A.   08

David was a boy with a wonderful imagination. When his teacher,
Mr. Sanderson, began describing Plymouth Colony and the first
Thanksgiving, David thought he could imagine just what being there
would have been like.

Mr. Sanderson said that in their search for religious freedom, the Pilgrims fled from England to Holland. Then, in the year 1620, they sailed all the way across the ocean to America on a ship called the *Mayflower*.

Going home on the school bus, David imagined he was arriving in Plymouth Harbor with the other Pilgrims. The voyage had been hard, but how exciting it was to be there at last!

Plymouth Harbor disappeared. The bus arrived at David's stop.

He imagined he was getting off in front of a small cottage, built during the first year of Plymouth Colony. It was made of wooden posts, sticks and straw mixed with clay, and rough wooden clapboards. It had a steep thatched roof and a chimney made of clay and sticks.

But the cottage disappeared, and there was David's house. It was big and white. Down the steps came David's father.

"David," he called, "come help me get the turkey for Grandma."

"Okay," said David.

David and his father walked toward the car.

"Dad," said David, "why do we eat turkey at Thanksgiving?"

"Well," said Dad, "your mom likes turkey, I like turkey, everybody likes turkey."

"But we don't know if the Pilgrims even had turkey at the first Thanksgiving. There's no proof."

"Well, we're having it anyway. Get in the car," said Dad.

David imagined he was off to hunt wild turkeys for the first
Thanksgiving. It was a lot more fun than going to the supermarket.
David steadied his musket as he entered the woods.

The car pulled into the shopping mall parking lot.

"Come on," said David's father. "Let's hurry."

They went into the supermarket. They walked down the long aisles filled with food.

"I bet the Pilgrims would have liked something like this," said Dad.

"I don't think so," said David. "I think they liked doing the harvesting themselves."

David imagined he was helping gather corn for the first Thanksgiving. The sun was shining, and everyone was happy.

Many Pilgrims had died during the past winter, but the survivors were well and the first harvest was bountiful. There was much to celebrate, much to be thankful for.

"Oh, David," said Dad, "pick out a can of cranberry sauce, would you please?"

David went to the shelf and picked out the smooth kind, the kind that slid out in a lump the shape of the can. He handed the can to his father.

"Hmmm," said Dad, "this is fine, but Grandma likes the whole berries. Better get one of those, too."

"The Pilgrims didn't even have cranberry sauce at the first Thanksgiving," said David.

"Never mind," said Dad. "*We're* having two kinds!"

When David and his father got home, Mom said,
"Hey, that's a great-looking turkey."
"I think so," said Dad.
"It's okay," said David.

"What's the matter, David?" asked
Mom. "Aren't you excited about
Thanksgiving?"

"I guess so," said David, "but it's
not going to be a *real* Thanksgiving.
Not like the Thanksgiving the
Pilgrims had."

"But everyone's coming," said
Mom. "Uncle Ned will do card tricks,
Aunt Marie's in from Omaha, and
don't you want to see your baby cousin
Katherine? Come on now. Help me get
the turkey ready."

But David wasn't convinced. As his mother bustled around the kitchen, he imagined her cooking in his Plymouth cottage. The fire was on stones under the chimney. They would keep the coals burning all night. Early tomorrow they would roast the turkey and turn it with the fire irons. What a feast there was going to be!

David's mother was wearing a cap, a white collar, and an apron over her long skirt. She had to be careful to keep her skirt out of the fire.

That night, as David was getting ready for bed, he couldn't help but think how much more exciting the first Thanksgiving must have been.

David woke up early in the morning. He imagined he was in a narrow bed on a mattress filled with straw. Across the cottage was one carved chair. There was one small table and a large trunk in a corner. He could smell the smoke from the cooking fire.

"David!" said his mother. "Breakfast's ready!"

David stopped imagining he was in Plymouth Colony. He pulled on his bathrobe and rushed to the den. His parents had already started eating. They were watching the Macy's Thanksgiving Day Parade on TV.

Yogi Bear and Mickey Mouse balloons floated by. "This is always so great," said Mom.

"Yeah," said David, happily sitting down to eggs and toast. "It's still not like the first Thanksgiving, though."

David imagined he heard the sound of marching feet. He looked out the window, and there was Captain Miles Standish, commander in chief of the Pilgrim army. He looked a lot like Mr. Sanderson. Behind him marched two lines of soldiers.

And around them the feast was just beginning. There were long tables piled with duck and goose and venison, with clams and corn bread—and wild plums for dessert. There were wrestling matches and races being run. Chief Massasoit and ninety of his braves were arriving to celebrate the peace made with Governor Bradford during the past year.

Oh, what a parade! Oh, what a Thanksgiving!

The Macy's Parade was over. David helped his parents clear the breakfast trays.

"Okay, David," said Dad when they were done. "Time to get dressed. We've got to be at Grandma's pretty soon."

"Do I have to wear my blue sweater?" David asked.

"Yes," said Mom, "it's cold out."

"But I hate that sweater. It itches, and it looks terrible."

"You won't have to wear it for long," said Mom, "and I think it looks terrific."

David went to his room. He couldn't stand that dumb blue sweater. He hated his shirt and pants and the good shoes that weren't anywhere near as comfortable as his sneakers.

He imagined he was back in Plymouth Colony, putting on a high-waisted jacket called a doublet and a white linen collar called a falling band. He put on his knee breeches and shoes. He looked fabulous!

When he was ready, it was time to walk two blocks and around a corner to Grandma's. David imagined he and his parents were walking through Plymouth Colony. On the right were newly harvested cornfields. On the left were two new cottages and a third that was almost finished.

They stopped and said hello to two Indians, Samoset and Squanto. Both spoke English. Squanto had shown the Pilgrims how to plant their corn and where to fish.

When David looked again, he was back on his own street. He saw
his neighbors' homes, each one with a lawn and garage. A new house
was almost complete.

The two Indians were really Jim Holden and his teenage son Jeff.
They lived three houses away.

When everyone was finished talking, Mom turned to David. "You
know what?" she said. "We forgot the carving board. Could you
please go back and get it?"

David ran home, but as he ran, he imagined he was in Plymouth Colony again. When he reached his door, he noticed a tall figure standing at the top of the hill behind the cottage.

David climbed up after him. The hill he was climbing was Fort Hill, overlooking Plymouth. The figure at the top was Captain Miles Standish. He was standing beside one of the five cannons. He was looking out beyond the colony. It was very beautiful.

The figure turned. It was Mr. Sanderson! And the wilderness beyond was David's own neighborhood.

"Hi," said Mr. Sanderson.

David had never seen his teacher out of school before. "Hi," he said, "why are you here?"

"Being up here makes me think of the first Thanksgiving."

"But the first Thanksgiving was so exciting."

"It probably wasn't any more exciting than ours. Times have changed, but we're thankful for the same things the Pilgrims were. Our homes, our friends, our families."

"I still think it would have been fun to be in Plymouth."

"It would have been, but Thanksgiving today is everything a Pilgrim boy would have wished for."

"Gee," said David, "I guess you're right. If a Pilgrim boy were here, I could even show him cranberry sauce!"

Mr. Sanderson smiled. "Happy Thanksgiving, David."

"Thanks, Mr. Sanderson. Happy Thanksgiving to you, too!"

David ran down the hill. He got the carving board and ran all the way to Grandma's.

Her house looked as nice as any cottage in Plymouth Colony. Grandma hugged him and led him inside.

"Happy Thanksgiving, Grandma!" said David, and meant it.

"Why, Happy Thanksgiving, David," said Grandma.

As they reached the dining room, everyone rose to greet them. But there was one unfamiliar guest. To David he looked exactly like a boy from Plymouth Colony.

"This is my neighbor, Michael," said Grandma. "His parents are away and he's spending Thanksgiving with us."

Everyone started talking. Everyone seemed to get along. Even baby cousin Katherine wasn't so bad. By the time the turkey was served, David and Michael were friends.

It turned out to be a great Thanksgiving. And David knew why. What Mr. Sanderson said was really true. Thanksgiving today wasn't so different from the very first one. It will always be a time for appreciating your friends and family, your home and your teacher. And we will always be thankful for being together.

David couldn't imagine anything better than that.